LUCKY ENOUGH

LUCKY ENOUGH

FRED BOWEN

FRED BOWEN
SPORTS STORY

Ω
PEACHTREE
ATLANTA

Published by
PEACHTREE PUBLISHERS
1700 Chattahoochee Avenue
Atlanta, Georgia 30318-2112
www.peachtree-online.com

Text © 2018 by Fred Bowen

Edited by Vicky Holifield
Design and composition by Melanie McMahon Ives

Printed in January 2018 in the United States of America by LSC
Communications in Harrisonburg, Virginia
10 9 8 7 6 5 4 3 2 1
First Edition
HC 978-1-56145-957-5
PB 978-1-56145-958-2

Library of Congress Cataloging-in-Publication Data

Names: Bowen, Fred, author.
Title: Lucky enough / written by Fred Bowen.
Description: First edition. | Atlanta, Georgia : Peachtree Publishers, 2018.
| Summary: Thirteen-year-old Trey, sure his lucky charm got him onto
the Ravens thirteen-year-old travel baseball team, becomes increasingly
superstitious and, when he loses the charm, he loses confidence, as well.
Identifiers: LCCN 2017015398| ISBN 9781561459575 (hardcover) | ISBN
9781561459582 (trade pbk.)
Subjects: | CYAC: Baseball—Fiction. | Superstition—Fiction. | Luck—
Fiction. | Self-confidence—Fiction. | Lost and found possessions—Fiction.
Classification: LCC PZ7.B6724 Luc 2018 | DDC [Fic]—dc23 LC record
available at https://lccn.loc.gov/2017015398

To the memory of my sister,
Margaret Bowen Decamp (1944–2017).
We were all lucky to know her.

CHAPTER 1

I cannot believe it! I can't find it!

I'm standing in the middle of my bedroom, all dressed and ready for the biggest day of my baseball career. Me—Trey Thompson—trying out for the Ravens, the thirteen-and-under travel team.

I really want to make it this time.

I didn't make it last year, and all season I had to listen to my best friend Cole McLaughlin brag about how great it was to be on the Ravens. There I was, still stuck on the Lookouts, the same old recreational league team we'd been on since fifth grade.

I'm wearing my best baseball pants and a red T-shirt, hoping the coaches will notice me. I got my hat, cleats, glove. I'm all ready to go except for one thing—the most important thing.

I've got to find it.

I go through the pockets in all my pants and toss them on the bed. Even though I've already looked there once, I search every inch of the top of my dresser. I lift up the pile of sports magazines and check in the Red Sox mug where I keep my collection of seashells, beach stones, and sea glass. I look behind the picture of my grandmother and me I have balanced against the dresser mirror.

Nothing.

I take a deep breath and try to think where I saw it last. I know I took it to school yesterday because I had a math test in Mrs. Ficca's class. I remember taking it out of my jeans pocket after school and putting it down in its usual spot on the dresser.

So where is it? I've got to find it. There's no way I'll make the Ravens without it.

My heart is pounding and my hands are sweating. That's not good. I've got to be cool, calm, and collected for the tryout.

I pace the room, scanning the floor and looking in every corner. Still nothing.

Maybe it fell under the dresser. I get down on my hands and knees and sweep my hand underneath. I feel something, but all I pull out is an old Jolly Rancher still in its wrapper, a couple of nickels, and a fistful of dust.

Pressing my face against the bottom drawer, I reach my whole arm in as far as I can. My fingers grasp something smooth and hard and I pull it out.

It's covered in dust, but I can see the familiar dark blue, almost violet color.

All right! My lucky sea glass.

I touch the smooth blue edges with my thumb and feel myself calming down. Now I'm ready to go to Crocker Field and make the Ravens...with the help of my lucky charm.

Today I'm going to need all the luck I can get.

CHAPTER 2

Thompson...Trey. Move over to short-stop." Coach DeLamielleure—everyone calls him Coach D—motions with his bat. "I want to see how you do over there."

I hustle over from second base and get into line with Cole and Malik Jones, the Ravens starting shortstop.

"Hey," Cole whispers. "You're moving up."

"You think so?"

"I know so," Cole continues in a low voice. "Coach D sees that you can play second, so now he wants to find out if you can handle shortstop. I'll bet he'll ask you to play third base next."

I look around Crocker Field. The baseball diamond is filled with kids hoping to make the Ravens. Some are shagging fly balls. Others are running sprints. A few guys are lined up at the batting cage.

"Heads up!" Coach D yells.

I'd better stop daydreaming and concentrate on fielding grounders.

The first ball skims across the infield grass. I scoop it up and throw to first base. A little low. The throw from shortstop is a lot longer than from second base.

"Take another!" the coach calls.

I range a few steps toward second base, field the ball cleanly, and throw to first, making sure my throw is higher and harder than usual. The first baseman catches it chest high. Right on the money.

"Good! Here comes another one."

This time the ball skips to my right. I backhand it, plant my right foot in the infield dirt, and fire the ball as hard as I can to first base.

"Good play!" Coach D shouts. "Malik, show him how to set his feet."

Malik pulls me out of the shortstop line. He's big for thirteen and he seems a lot more confident than the rest of us—Cole says he's the best player on the Ravens. I believe it.

Malik starts right in. "Listen, Trey. Short-stop's a lot harder than second base. You got to field the ball clean and get rid of it quick."

He gets down in a fielder's position. "Try to field the ball coming in. Don't let the ball play you. If you can, field it with your right foot slightly in front of your left foot. That way, you're ready to step into your throw to first right away. Watch me."

Malik moves to the front of the line of players hoping to play infield for the Ravens. He steps into a three-hopper, fielding it just above his knees. Sure enough, his right foot is in front and his left is in back. He throws a strike across the diamond.

"Okay, Trey, you're up," Malik says.

I snag a high bouncer, but I'm thinking so much about where my feet are supposed to be that my throw sails high.

"Get the ball down!" Coach shouts. "Take another."

This time I forget about my feet and peg a perfect throw to first base.

"Good," Malik says. "Don't worry too much about shortstop. I'll probably be playing there all year."

I give him a look and go to the back of the line. I reach into my pocket and close my fingers around my blue sea glass. The smooth surface calms me down a little.

"Trey!" Coach D points the bat again. "Take a few grounders over at third base."

I trade glances with Cole. Maybe he's right. Coach wants to see if I can play all the infield positions.

After a few grounders at third base—I can definitely field from that spot—Coach calls out more orders. "Malik, Cole, and Trey, go to the batting cage and take some swings."

I fall into step with Cole.

"Good job," he says. "You showed Coach D you can handle shortstop *or* third base if he needs you. That'll help your chances, big time."

I grab Cole by the arm.

"What are you doing?" he asks, looking at me like I'm crazy.

I point at his foot that's just inches from the third-base chalk line. "Don't step on the foul line."

"Why?"

"It's bad luck," I explain. "No way I'll make the team if you go stepping on baselines."

"You're nuts," he says. But I notice he steps over it.

I examine the row of bats and try to decide which one has the most hits in it. I finally pick a red and black Rawlings model and take a short swing. It feels like the right length and weight. I take out the blue sea glass and, after I make sure no one is looking, run the edge of the glass along the barrel of the bat. Now I'm ready.

When it's my turn, I push back the heavy rope net and step into the cage and up to the plate. Mr. Locke, the batting coach, is behind an L-shaped screen with a bucket of baseballs.

"I'm throwing hard, so be ready," he says.

I make sure that I touch the four corners of the plate—first the two inside, then the two outside—with the tip of my bat for more good luck. Then I look out at Coach Locke.

The first pitch is a belt-high fastball—right where I like it. I uncoil a swing that rockets the ball right up the middle. Coach Locke ducks even though he's behind the screen.

"Whoa! Good hit," he says with an approving nod.

I keep the hits coming, spraying line drives all over the cage. The red and black Rawlings bat is like magic. I feel great.

I can't help smiling when Coach Locke says, "Okay, let's get another hitter in there. I don't want you wasting all those hits."

Later, Cole and I see Coach D and Coach Locke talking.

"Bet you a buck they're talking about you," Cole says.

"You think so?"

"I know so."

"Think I'll make it?" I'm not 100 percent sure. Or even 50 percent. You never know what's going to happen.

Cole shrugs. He isn't sure either. "Hard to say. It's partly a numbers game. They can only take a few new players." He looks around at all the kids trying out. "Too bad you can't pitch. They're always looking for pitchers. But you hit well and you showed you could play a bunch of different positions. You definitely have a good chance."

I hope he's right.

CHAPTER 3

No way I can study. I look at my World History textbook again, but it's like all those words about World War II won't come into focus.

Coach D said he would post the list of the kids who made the team within twenty-four hours. I've checked the Ravens website a million times since the tryout and nothing yet. It's now been almost twenty-seven hours.

My mom sticks her head in my bedroom. "How's the homework going?"

"Okay, I guess."

She gives me a sympathetic look. "Nothing posted yet?" she asks.

I shake my head.

"Don't worry." She smooths the hair on the

back of my head. "You did your best. That's all you can do. Now it's up to the coaches."

"I know." But knowing that doesn't make the wait easier.

"Remember, lights out by 9:30," she says as she closes the bedroom door.

My mom is usually pretty cool, but she worries about me too much. It's just the two of us in the apartment. My parents got divorced when I was around five.

My dad's in California now and has a new family. We don't see or hear much from him. I guess some people would say I haven't been very lucky, not having a dad around and all. But it's the only kind of life I can remember.

I put my books aside and go to my dresser. I pick up the blue sea glass and rub the smooth surface. I remember the day I found it like it was just last week.

I'm seven years old and I'm holding my grandmother's hand. We're walking along the shore near the beach house where she lives. She's talking. My grandmother is always talking.

"We're hunting for treasure, Trey," she says. "We've got to keep our eyes open. Sea glass can be hiding anywhere."

The late afternoon tide is out. The sand is soft and cool. My feet sink in, making it hard to walk.

"Oh, look at this." My grandmother reaches down and digs her fingers into the sand. She pulls out what looks like a small green stone.

"My, oh my," she says, turning the sea glass in her hand. "It's like an emerald."

"How do they make sea glass?" I ask.

My grandmother smiles. I can tell she likes it when I ask questions. She stares out at the waves rolling in.

"The ocean makes the sea glass. A bottle falls from a boat into the water or is swept away from shore by the tide. The waves toss it against the rocks and break it up. Then the water pushes the pieces of glass over the sand again and again for months, years—for who knows how long—smoothing out the jagged edges. Then one day the tide brings it up onto the beach for sharp-eyed treasure hunters like you and me to find."

She holds the green sea glass up to the light. A bunch of sea gulls skitter along the sand and take off, their wings cutting into the wind.

"It's wonderful how Mother Nature can take something so useless and ugly as a broken bottle and turn it into something so beautiful."

She drops the green sea glass into my red plastic bucket with our other treasures: small stones, shells, and several other pieces of sea glass.

I keep walking and searching along the shore. There must be a million little stones scattered on the wet sand.

Then my eye catches on something deep blue, like the blue-violet crayon in the Crayola box. My favorite color. I wonder if the fading afternoon light is playing tricks on me.

"Grandma!" I call, reaching down. "I think I found a blue one."

"Blue? Really?" I can hear the excitement in her voice. "You're lucky to find blue. You almost never find blue sea glass around here."

I dig it out and wash it off in the shallow water. I run to show her. The sea glass sparkles in the sun.

"Oh my goodness! This is beautiful, Trey. I don't think I've ever seen a better one."

I hold the blue sea glass tight in my hand, proud of my discovery. I don't want to put it in the bucket with the others. It feels too lucky, too special for that.

My grandmother looks at the sky. The sun is ducking in and out of the thickening clouds.

"Storm coming in tonight," she says. "We might as well head back to the house anyway. We'll never find anything more beautiful than your blue one."

We clamber over the rocks. It's a short walk on the sea wall and the shore road. We wash the sand off our feet in her front yard with a garden hose and slip past the sign out front that says At the Beach and into a house filled with pictures, books, and light.

"Do you want some ice water?"

"Sure."

I look out the big kitchen window to the ocean. The water's darker now that the sun is sinking and the clouds are rolling in. There's another sign hanging above the window. I can read it without any help:

If you are lucky enough to live near the sea, you are lucky enough.

My blue sea glass is still in my hand. My grandmother brings me my water. She hugs me. Her bathing suit is still wet but her arms are warm. Her gray hair smells of ocean salt.

"I am so lucky to have you as a grandson," she whispers. "So lucky...."

I take a deep breath and look at the clock on my nightstand. It says 9:15. I'll check the Ravens site one more time before I go to bed.

I open my laptop. A new screen pops up. My heart jumps into my throat.

Announcement: The following players are requested to report to the Ravens first practice at Crocker Field at 5 p.m. on Wednesday, March 28.

JOSHUA BERTELLI
JAYDEN CLARK
DYLAN DIAZ
WALLACE DRAVES
ANTHONY HANSEN
MALIK JONES
CAMERON KELLY
ALEX KIM
MASON LONG
COLE MCLAUGHLIN
PETER RODRIGUEZ
TREY THOMPSON
JAMES WALKER
NOAH WASHINGTON

I can't read the rest of the announcement. I'm too excited about being on the Ravens. My phone buzzes. It's a text from Cole.

Welcum to Ravens. D dn take many new kids. U r lucky u made it.

Lucky. I rub my blue sea glass again. That's exactly how I feel.

CHAPTER 4

We turn into the parking lot next to Crocker Field. "When will practice be over?" my mother asks.

"Coach said two hours."

"Okay. I'll swing by and pick you guys up at 7 p.m."

Cole and I pop out of the car. I'm excited and ready to go.

"Be sure to drink plenty of water!" my mother calls as she drives away. "Love you."

We've hardly put our water bottles down when Coach D shouts, "Trey, go to the batting cage! Cole, go to the outfield to shag flies! Let's move it. Everybody hustles on the field."

I search through the bats on the rack. "Where's that Rawlings bat?" I ask. "You know, the red one with the black handle?"

"That wasn't one of the team bats," Peter Rodriguez, the Ravens starting catcher, explains. "It belonged to that kid who got cut. I think his name was Jay."

"You're kidding me!" I cry out. "Man, I loved that bat. It had a million hits in it."

Peter doesn't feel my pain. "What do you care? Just grab any bat. They all work." Then he proves his point by smashing Coach Locke's pitching all over the cage.

I go back to studying the bats. I pick a Mizuno model and hope it's as good as the red and black Rawlings.

No such luck. It's okay, but I'm nowhere near the line-drive machine I was at tryouts. Coach Locke is full of batting suggestions as he keeps firing fastballs.

"Have your bat ready!" he calls. "Be on time."

He sends me another fastball. "Let me see your best bat speed. Swing like you mean it!"

I manage a few weak flies and grounders, but basically the batting session is a big disappointment.

Afterwards, I walk out of the cage with my head down and toss the bat back onto the rack. If only that kid Jay had forgotten his Rawlings bat and left it here. I just couldn't hit a thing with that stupid Mizuno bat.

I look around. Everyone is hitting, fielding, pitching, or running. No one is standing around. Coach D runs a real tight practice. This Ravens team is serious business.

I don't mind. As one of the new guys, I know I'm going to have to bust my butt every second of practice to show that I belong.

With about forty minutes left to go, Coach D shouts, "All right, let's scrimmage!" He splits everyone into two teams. It looks like he's trying to make the teams even by mixing the new guys in with the players from last year. None of that first-team, second-team stuff. I'm playing second base with Malik at shortstop and Cole in left field. Coach Locke pitches for both teams.

Waiting in the on-deck circle for my first at-bat, I reach into my pocket and take out the blue sea glass. I rub it along the length of the Easton bat I picked out this time. Maybe it will get me some hits.

When I step into the batter's box, I touch the four corners of the plate with the tip of the bat.

"Come on," sneers Peter from his position as catcher. "Be a hitter. Get in the box."

The first pitch streaks by. Strike one.

"Your magic mojo not working today?" Peter taunts.

I let two high pitches go by and foul off another fastball. Two balls, two strikes.

The next pitch is outside and low. I hold off. Full count—three balls, two strikes. Nobody's on base and there are two outs, so I figure Coach will not want to walk me. I remind myself to be ready and get my bat going.

A belt-high fastball steams in.

Crack! A line drive shoots over the second baseman's head.

I bolt out of the batter's box, convinced that I can get two bases out of this one. Sure enough, Coach D waves me around first. I sprint past the bag and head for second. The shortstop is waiting for the throw. I know it's going to be close as I start my head-first slide. My hands smack into the base just as the shortstop slams his glove into my side.

"Safe!" Coach D calls.

I hop up and slap the dirt off my shirt and baseball pants.

"Good hustle, Trey!" Coach D turns to the rest of the players. "That's what I want to see this year. Everybody running hard right out of the batter's box on every play."

I feel great standing on second base. I feel even better when Cole knocks me in with a clean single to center. My stretching a single into two bases means we score a run.

In the field I make a couple of routine plays at second. No problem. Later, with two outs and runners on second and third, Peter scorches a sinking line drive out to second base. Without thinking, I flash the leather and scoop the hard one-hopper off the infield dirt.

I'm almost surprised to find the ball in my glove. I toss the ball to get Peter for the final out of the inning. He slams his batting helmet against the infield grass.

I can't resist. "Maybe you should try touching all four corners of the plate next at-bat," I tell Peter as I jog past him. "You know, for good luck."

Our bench is alive with high fives and excited talk.

"Great play, Trey! How we pick it!"

"Web gem. Call ESPN!"

"Good defense! You saved a couple runs."

A hit, a run, and a sweet pick at second. I'm starting to feel like I'm part of the Ravens now.

After practice, Coach D hands out the uniforms. They look cool. Dark blue hats, blue socks, dark blue shirts with white letters and trim. Real big league. Way better than the Lookouts purple T-shirts.

I get number 6 but start scouting around for number 14. I wore it my first year on the

Lookouts and played well, so I made sure I got my number 14 every season after that.

Big problem. Peter has my lucky number. Still, I want it so badly I walk right up to him.

"You want to trade shirts?" I ask. "Fourteen's my favorite number."

Peter gives me a look. "Favorite bats? Favorite numbers?" His voice is a little too loud, like he's talking to everyone else on the team. "Takes you all day just to get into the batter's box. You sure got a lot of weird ways of playing, Thompson."

He holds out the shirt.

I reach for it.

He jerks it back. "What's it worth to you?" he asks.

"What do you mean?"

"If you want the number so bad, maybe you should pay me for it." A small smile slides across his face.

"I don't have—I mean—" I don't feel like explaining to this guy that my family's not rich. He already thinks I'm weird. "You know what? Just forget it."

Peter tosses the shirt at me. "Go on. Take it. I was just messing with you," he says. "The number doesn't mean anything to me. A real ballplayer doesn't need any special number to play."

CHAPTER 5

O kay, let's move fast," Mom says as we walk into the apartment. "Remember, you have to study for that World War II history test tomorrow."

"No worries. I don't have any other homework tonight." I drop my baseball equipment bag on the sofa.

"Come on, Trey," she scolds. "Don't leave your stuff there."

I pick up the bag and take it to my room. "Hey, Mom!" I call. "Do we have any pizza?"

"I can't hear you," Mom says from the kitchen. "If you want to talk to me come in here."

When I get to the kitchen, I open the freezer and consider the possibilities. "How about pepperoni pizza tonight?"

"Okay, but you need to eat some salad, too."

"All right. All right."

We snap into action like a couple of major leaguers turning the double play. I start the oven and put the pizza on a big cookie sheet. Mom washes the lettuce and cuts up the cucumbers and carrots.

As I take down two plates from the cabinet, I notice my grandmother's sign above the sink.

If you are lucky enough to live near the sea, you are lucky enough.

Two years ago, not long after my grandmother died, my mom brought the sign here from the beach house. She hung it just above the window over our kitchen sink. It's sort of a joke since it overlooks the parking lot of our apartment complex. We must be more than a hundred miles from the ocean.

"What kind of test will it be?" Mom asks.

"Multiple choice. Ms. Ko gave us a study packet with fifty questions and answers about World War II. She'll pick twenty for the test."

"Doesn't sound too tough."

"You don't know Ms. Ko."

The timer sounds and I pull the pizza from the oven. I cut it into slices and put one on each plate.

"Do you have the questions?"

"Yeah."

"Good. Run and get them so I can quiz you during dinner."

When I come back with my history study packet, Mom is putting the salad in two bowls.

"Do we have any soda?" I ask.

Mom shakes her head. "Too expensive. And besides, soda is nothing but carbonated sugar water." She slides a tall glass of water to me. "Drink this. It's cheaper and it's good for you."

While I pour the dressing on my salad, Mom looks over the history questions. "Are you ready?" she asks. "What country did both Germany and the Soviet Union invade to start World War II?"

I take a bite of pizza. The hot cheese burns the roof of my mouth. "Ow!" I say, reaching for my glass of water. I'm off to a bad start.

"Um...France?" I mumble.

She stares at me.

"I mean...Belgium?"

"Come on, Trey. You're just guessing," she says with a slight shake of her head. "It was Poland. Germany attacked from the west and the Soviet Union attacked from the east. Okay, I'll give you a chance to redeem yourself. What year did they attack?"

"In 1941?"

"I thought you said you studied this stuff!"

"I was going to." I put another slice of pizza on my plate and pop a circle of pepperoni into my mouth.

"September 1, 1939. Be sure to eat your salad." She sighs. "Okay. Who was the leader of Nazi Germany?"

"That's easy. Adolf Hitler."

"Name two allies of Germany during World War II."

"Italy and...ah...give me a hint."

"Will Ms. Ko give you a hint?"

"Kind of. I mean it's a multiple choice test."

"Okay, one hint. This country attacked the United States at Pearl Harbor."

"Japan!"

My mother gives me a look and pushes the study packet across the table. "You'd better study more before you go to bed, young man."

"I did pretty good," I protest.

"*Well*," my mother says, correcting my grammar. "You did pretty *well*. But remember: Good, better, best—"

"I know, I know. 'Good, better, best. Never let them rest until your good is better and your better is best.'" That's one of my grandma's sayings. I've heard it a million times.

"That's right." Mom dismisses me with a wave of her hand. "Now get to work. Don't worry, I'll do the dishes tonight."

I walk into my room, flop down on the bed, and start looking over the questions.

Q: Who was the Prime Minister of the United Kingdom who signed the Munich Agreement thinking it would bring "peace in our time"?

A: Neville Chamberlain

Q: The Munich Agreement allowed Nazi Germany to annex portions of what country?

A: Czechoslovakia

I grab my glove and begin to toss a baseball toward the ceiling. The first Ravens practice went great except for the fact that Peter thinks I'm some kind of weirdo because of all my superstitions. He would really give me a hard time if he knew about my lucky sea glass.

The ball bounces off the heel of my glove and klonks against the floor.

"Timothy Andrew Thompson!" my mother calls from the kitchen. "Are you studying in there?"

"Don't worry, Mom! I'm memorizing the leaders of the Allied nations." I take another look at the packet. I shut my eyes and try to name them. Joseph Stalin is the leader of the Soviet Union. Franklin D. Roosevelt, the United States. Winston Churchill, England.

Looking at all the names reminds me of a baseball lineup. That gets me thinking about the Ravens again. I jump off the bed and turn on my laptop. With a few clicks I'm on the Ravens website, looking at their spring schedule.

Ravens Season Schedule
All Home Games Played at Crocker Field

Coach Robert DeLamielleure

Date	Opponent	Location and Time
Sat. April 7	Chiefs	Home – 2:00 p.m.
Tues. April 10	Red Wings	Away – 5:30 p.m.
Sat. April 14	Aces (DH)	Away – noon
Wed. April 18	Grizzlies	Home – 5:30 p.m.
Sat. April 21	Tides (DH)	Home – 11:00 a.m.
Tues. April 24	Bisons	Away – 5:30 p.m.
Sat. April 28	Zephyrs (DH)	Away – noon
Tues. May 1	Clippers	Home – 5:30 p.m.
Sat. May 5	Redbirds (DH)	Away – 1:00 p.m.
Tues. May 8	Aces	Home – 5:30 p.m.
Thurs. May 10	Tides	Away – 6:00 p.m.
Sat. May 12	Chiefs (DH)	Away – 1:00 p.m.

Wed. May 16	Bisons	Home – 5:30 p.m.
Sat. May 19	Grizzlies (DH)	Away – 11:00 a.m.
Tues. May 22	Zephyrs	Home – 5:30 p.m.
Sat. May 26	Red Wings (DH)	Home – noon
Wed. May 29	Clippers	Away – 6:00 p.m.
June 6–10	Playoffs	TBA

I print it out and tuck it into the corner of the mirror above my dresser. I grab my phone and text Cole.

Can't w8 for r 1st game Sat

A message buzzes back in no time.

Chiefs r pretty good

I glance over at the blue sea glass on my dresser. I can almost hear my grandmother saying, "Good, better, best...."

I go back to studying about World War II. I've got less than an hour to learn all this stuff for the test. I think I'll take my lucky sea glass to school tomorrow.

Just in case.

CHAPTER 6

So who do you think will start at second base tomorrow?" I ask Cole as we walk into Thurgood Marshall Middle School. The front hallway is filled with chattering sixth, seventh, and eighth graders and the clatter of slamming locker doors.

"Coach D will probably play Mason Long at second."

Even though Cole is almost shouting, I can barely hear him.

"He played that position last year." Cole looks over at me. "I mean, Coach likes you, but not *that* much."

"Think he'll play me at all?" This is what

I'm really worried about. I think I've done pretty well in the practices, but you never know. I really don't want to get stuck on the bench.

"Sure. He'll probably play you about half the game at either second or third," Cole says. "Don't worry. Coach D is good about giving kids playing time."

"Keep moving, people!" our vice principal Ms. McIntyre shouts above the noise. "You only have sixty seconds to get to your class!"

"Did you study for Ko's test?" Cole asks as we turn into our hallway, where it's a little quieter.

"Yeah, but I hope she picks some easy questions."

I'm not kidding when I say that. I memorized as much as I could, but I didn't have time to study everything in the packet. I'll have to get lucky on some of the questions.

I sit down at my desk next to Veronica Valdez. She's super smart. Veronica is a lock to get a 100 percent on the test. She probably studies in her sleep.

When Ms. Ko steps into class, she's all

business. She has her real teacher voice going. "Everything off your desk except a blue or black pen. As soon as I hand out the tests, place them facedown on your desk. Do not turn them over until I tell you to do so."

I stare at the back of the test and start to get nervous. I wish I'd studied more. I reach into my pocket and pull out my lucky sea glass. I rub it with my right thumb while Ms. Ko gives her final instructions.

"You will have twenty minutes to complete the test. Read each question carefully and make sure you understand it. Then read *all* the choices before you make a decision. Circle the letter you think is the right one. When you are done with the test, go back and check your work."

"What if you want to change an answer?" someone asks from the back of the room.

"Put an X through your first answer and then put a circle around your second answer." Ms. Ko looks around the room. "Any other questions?"

Veronica looks like she can't wait to start.

"You may begin," says Ms. Ko.

I turn my test over. I have my pen in my right hand and my sea glass in my left. I know the first two answers, no problem.

1. What two countries did Nazi Germany annex before the beginning of World War II?

(a.) Czechoslovakia and Austria
b. Poland and France
c. Czechoslovakia and Italy
d. Austria and Spain

2. What country did both Nazi Germany and the Soviet Union attack on September 1, 1939, to begin World War II?

a. France
b. Czechoslovakia
(c.) Poland
d. United States

I'm off to a good start.

But as I move on, the questions get harder. I can narrow down most of the answers to a couple of choices, but I have to guess on a few. By the end of the test, I'm rubbing the sea glass so hard my thumb hurts. Looks like my grade will depend on how well my lucky charm works on history tests and how good a guesser I am.

"One minute to go," Ms. Ko warns. "Make your final decisions. Check your work."

I put the sea glass in my pocket and look back over some of the harder questions. I start to change one answer, but then decide to stick with the one I've got.

"Pens down."

I hear a few moans from kids who obviously haven't finished. Ms. Ko walks between the desks handing out red pencils. "Rows one and two exchange papers. Rows three and four do the same."

I hand my paper to Veronica and she gives me hers. Ms. Ko goes through the questions, using the occasion to explain more about World War II.

I glance over from time to time to see if Veronica is making a lot of marks on my test. I can't figure out how well I did even when I hear the right answers. It's weird how hard it is to remember which ones you chose when you had to guess.

After she finishes, Ms. Ko tells us to tally all the incorrect answers and subtract 5 percent for each one that is wrong. "Put the percentage at the top of the page," she says. "If you have trouble figuring out the score, you shouldn't be in seventh grade."

Sure enough, Veronica nails all twenty questions. I don't know why Ms. Ko even gave me a red pencil. I'm never going to put a single red mark on that girl's tests.

I mark a big red 100 percent on Veronica's paper. When I take my test from her, my hands are shaking. It's the moment of truth. Mom will be real disappointed if I get anything below a B.

I peek at the top of the page and let out a big sigh of relief. Eighty-five percent isn't too bad. I look over the test. Three of my guesses came through…big time. I was super lucky. If those guesses had been wrong I would have barely made a C.

It looks as if my lucky sea glass works in history class as well as it does on the baseball diamond.

CHAPTER 7

"Trey, get over there and start swinging a bat!" Coach D calls down the bench. "You're going to pinch hit for Mason this inning and then play second."

Cole nudges me in the ribs. "What did I tell you?" he says, sitting a little taller on the bench. "You're gonna play half the game at second or third."

I look at the scoreboard.

INNING	1	2	3	4	5	6	7
Chiefs	1	0	0	1			
Ravens	1	0	3				

The Ravens are ahead 4–2 in the bottom of the fourth in a seven-inning game.

"Hansen...Clark!" Coach calls out. "And Thompson! Let's get some hits. We need some more runs."

I grab my new favorite Easton bat and take a few swings. I hope it has at least one hit in it today.

Hansen strikes out and Clark pops a fly to the shortstop. Two outs, nobody on. I step into the batter's box and touch the four corners of the plate. A fastball at the knees sizzles in.

Strike one!

Whoa, the pitchers in the travel league definitely throw faster than the kids on the Lookouts. I foul off the second pitch. Two strikes.

"Get the bat started!" Coach Locke yells from the first-base coach's box. The Chiefs pitcher tries to tempt me with a high fast-ball. I hold back. The next pitch is in the dirt. Two balls, two strikes.

Be ready, I tell myself. *He's going to come*

in with one. He doesn't want to walk me and face Malik.

For a moment, I think about the sea glass in my pocket because I could use a little luck right now, then I focus on the pitcher again.

Another fastball. I'm a little late but I get the barrel of the bat on the ball. A line drive streaks over the second baseman's head for a clean single. I almost dance to first base.

The Ravens bench is alive, and Cole's leading the cheers.

"Way to go, Trey!"

"Good at-bat!"

"How to get it started!"

"Two outs," Coach Locke reminds me. "Running hard on anything."

Malik lashes a line drive into the right center-field gap. I'm off, sprinting around second to third base. Coach D waves me home. I touch the inside corner of the bag and turn on the jets. I see the Chiefs catcher waiting for the ball at home plate. Cole is pushing his hands down, signaling me to slide.

I hit the dirt, hooking my left foot along the edge of the plate just as the catcher slaps the tag on my back.

"Safe!" The umpire calls, spreading his arms wide.

I jump up and punch my fist into the air. We're ahead, 5–2. A bunch of Ravens parents burst into cheers. My mom's not in the stands today because she had to work.

We score another run on a hit by Cole. So we are leading 6–2 when I step over the foul line to take my place at second base.

I toe the infield dirt and secretly hope I get an easy play or two to settle my nerves. No such luck.

Crack!

A hot shot comes skidding between first and second base. I take a couple of quick steps to my left, angling onto the outfield grass. With my last step I leap out and snag the ball in my outstretched glove. I scramble to my knees and throw to first.

Out!

All the Ravens are cheering again. I think I even impressed Malik with that play.

"Call Sports Center!"

"Great defense."

Everything keeps going great. I learn that my Easton bat has another hit in it when I lash another line drive single in the sixth inning. I make two more plays at second. Nothing as spectacular as the first, but at least I don't mess up.

Most important, we win 9–3.

I'm walking out of the dugout when Coach Locke asks, "Do you want to see the box score?"

"Sure."

He spins his computer toward me.

Ravens	AB	R	H	RBI
Clark CF	4	2	2	1
Long 2B	2	0	0	0
Thompson 2B	2	1	2	1
Jones SS	4	2	3	3
McLaughlin LF	4	1	1	1
Rodriguez C	3	1	2	1
Draves 1B	2	1	1	1
Diaz 1B	1	0	0	0
Bertelli 3B	3	1	1	0

Kim RF	2	0	1	0
Kelly RF	1	0	0	0
Hansen P	2	0	0	0
Washington P	0	0	0	0
Walker P	1	0	0	0
Totals	31	9	13	8

"Two for two at the plate, a run scored," Coach Locke says, eyeing the screen. "And a starred play in the field. Nice start. If you keep it up, you'll be playing a lot."

"Thanks, I was just lucky."

Coach Locke smiles. "I'm not so sure about that. You looked like you belonged out there."

*****

I walk into the apartment still flying high from the Ravens win and my two hits.

"How was the game?" Mom is sitting on the living room sofa in front of her laptop.

"Great!" I realize that I'm almost screaming and try to tone it down a little. "I played half the game and got two hits. I even made

a super play in the hole to get a guy at first!"
I go through the motions of throwing the
ball to first base. "Coach Locke said if I keep
playing like that I'll definitely be starting
soon."

"All right!" Mom exclaims.

We trade high fives. "Maybe we should
celebrate," she says. "I've got about fifteen,
twenty minutes of work left. Then we can go
out and get some real pizza at Bertucci's."

"Sounds great. I'll even order some salad."

"It's a deal." Mom looks back at the screen.
"Why don't you clean up and get changed
while I finish this report."

I go into my room and write the score on
the schedule, still replaying my first game
for the Ravens in my head. My lucky sea
glass really did the job today.

I take off my shirt and baseball pants.
They'll definitely need to go in the wash. I
reach into my pants pocket for my sea glass.

It's not there!

I check the back pockets. Empty.

Maybe...maybe I didn't take it to the
game.

No, I remember putting it in my pocket… for good luck. No way I would have gone to my first Ravens game without it.

But just to be sure, I check the top of my dresser. I grab the mug of sea glass and stones from the beach and dump them out on my bed. I see green, brown, gray, but no blue.

I search through my uniform pockets one more time. Still empty. Just in case I dropped it like last time, I kneel and swipe my hand under the dresser. Nothing.

I plop down on the edge of the bed, scattering the sea glass and stones. It's like I'm frozen or something. I can't move. I'm just thinking…*where could it be? What am I going to do if I can't find it?*

My mom sticks her head in the room. "Is my star baseball player ready for some real pizza?"

I look up. I had forgotten all about going out to Bertucci's.

"Come on, I thought you were getting cleaned up. Get a decent shirt on," she says then gives me a strange look. "Are you okay?"

"I'm fine," I say. "Maybe just a little tired from the game."

She puts her hand on my forehead. Whenever she does that it makes me feel like a little kid.

"No fever," she says and then taps my forehead lightly with her knuckles like she's knocking on a door. "Bertucci's...real pizza... remember?"

"I remember." I smile weakly.

After my mom leaves the room, I grab my phone and text Cole.

Can u meet me @ Crocker tomorrow? 9 am

Sure, whassup?

Tell u tomorrow

CHAPTER 8

So when was the last time you saw it?"

Cole and I are standing near home plate at Crocker Field. The Sunday morning sun is halfway up the sky and it's already getting hot.

"When I put it in my pocket before the game against the Chiefs," I say, picturing myself putting on my uniform.

"Which pocket?"

"I don't know. What does it matter?"

"If you put it in your back pocket, it could have fallen out when you were sliding home." Cole takes a quick look around home plate.

I stand there thinking for a moment. "I'm pretty sure I put it in one of my front pockets."

"In that case," Cole says, "maybe it fell out when you were sitting on the bench or when you were taking your batting gloves out of your pocket." He's starting to sound like one of those detectives on TV.

I look around the field hopelessly. "It could be anywhere."

"Let's check around the bench first," Cole suggests.

"Okay." I point to the third-base side. "We were over there. Remember, it's about an inch long and it's dark blue."

Cole gives me a look. "I know. I've seen it a million times. You carry it everywhere."

The dugout is cool and shaded from the sun. I get down on my hands and knees and edge along behind the bench, poking into the dirt with my fingers, hoping against hope that the sea glass is there. Cole walks the length of the bench staring at the ground.

"Any luck?" Cole asks.

"Nope. How about you?"

Cole shakes his head.

I sink down on the bench. "Man, we've got to find it. I got two hits with it on Saturday."

"Wait a minute. When did you lose it?" Cole asks.

"Jeez. If I knew that we would have found it by now."

"Then how do you know you didn't get your hits *after* you lost your lucky sea glass?"

Cole is sounding like that TV detective again. I have to admit he has a point, but it doesn't make me feel any better. I look out on the baseball field. It looks bigger than usual.

"We need to look over the whole field."

"Why?" Cole sounds like I stuck him with a pin. "Why the whole field? You only played infield."

"Yeah, but we warmed up in the outfield before the game, remember? I could have lost it then." I get up, walk over to the backstop, and point down the first-base line to the right-field fence about eighty yards away.

"I'll walk to the fence looking on both sides of me," I say, explaining my plan. "You walk beside me about ten feet away and do the same thing. When we get to the fence, we'll move over and walk back. That way we'll eventually cover the whole field."

"Come on, Trey. There's no way we'll ever find it."

I know Cole's probably right, but I don't want to give up hope just yet. "Sure we can. I found it when it was on the beach hiding among a million rocks."

"Okay. But you do know you're acting a little crazy, right? It's just a piece of blue glass."

That stings a little, but I ignore him and start trudging down the field, looking from side to side. He hesitates for a few seconds, then joins me in the search.

The sun gets higher and we get hotter. When we get to the outfield, Cole complains, "The grass is awfully thick out here."

"Just keep looking."

We're almost to the third-base line when someone calls out, "What are you boys doing out there staring at the ground?"

The groundskeeper at Crocker Field is dressed in baggy pants and a blue work shirt with holes at the elbows. A battered Boston Red Sox hat is pulled down tight on his head, his shaggy gray hair sticking out around the edges. There are gray whiskers on his chin.

"Hey, Mr. Kiley. I lost something yesterday," I explain. "We're looking for it." I shift my weight from one foot to the other and glance at Cole.

"What did you lose?"

"A piece of blue sea glass."

Mr. Kiley raises an eyebrow and gives me a look. "What's so important about a piece of sea glass?"

I wish he'd stop asking questions and help us look. "I don't know. I just need it."

"Is it supposed to be lucky or something?" Mr. Kiley asks as he walks closer.

"Sort of."

Mr. Kiley nods. "You baseball players are a superstitious bunch. Lucky bats, lucky numbers. Doing all kinds of weird stuff before you get up to bat. Not touching the baseline—"

"Hey, *he* does that!" Cole points at me.

Mr. Kiley takes off his cap and slicks back his sweaty hair. "Ever hear of Willie Mays?" he asks, putting the cap back on.

"Sure." Cole and I go back to searching for the sea glass.

"Mays used to touch second base every time he ran out to his position in center field," Mr. Kiley says. "I guess he thought it helped him to be the great Willie Mays. Seems kind of silly if you ask me."

We keep searching and Mr. Kiley keeps talking. "Then there was Wade Boggs, a great third baseman for the Red Sox and Yankees. Man, he could hit. They used to call him 'the Chicken Man.'"

"Why'd they call him that?" I ask.

"He used to eat chicken before every game. Must have worked, too. He got around two hundred hits and a hundred walks a season for years."

Mr. Kiley eyes me more closely. "What's your name?"

"Timothy Andrew Thompson. But everybody calls me Trey."

"Oh yeah," Mr. Kiley says with a smile. "The new kid on the Ravens. You got two hits yesterday. Am I right?"

I nod. Hearing that Mr. Kiley noticed

my two hits makes me feel good.

"So you think that piece of sea glass helped you get those hits?" Mr. Kiley continues.

"Yeah...kind of," I say barely above a whisper.

The groundskeeper shakes his head. "Ever hear of Babe Ruth?"

"Why? Was he superstitious, too?" Cole asks.

"Not really. The Babe said he only had one superstition: 'I always touch all the bases after I hit a home run.' He hit 714 of them."

Mr. Kiley looks at his watch. "You boys better get out of here. I have to get the field ready for some games this afternoon."

"Mr. Kiley, if you find my—"

"Don't worry, son," Mr. Kiley says. "If I find your lucky sea glass, I'll get it back to you. What's it look like?"

I hold up my thumb and finger an inch apart. "It's about this long and real deep blue color."

"I'll keep an eye out for it. It'll probably turn up when I'm working on the field."

"Thanks."

"No problem. Now get going. And get some more hits."

"Think he'll find it?" Cole asks.

"I sure hope so."

Cole and I walk away. I make extra sure I step over the baseline.

CHAPTER 9

I'm standing in my uniform in front of my
dresser. I look at the Ravens schedule.

Date	Opponent	Location and Time
Sat. April 7	Chiefs W 9-3	Home – 2:00 p.m.
Tues. April 10	Red Wings W 6-4	Away – 5:30 p.m.
Sat. April 14	Aces (DH) L 4-2	Away – noon
Wed. April 18	Grizzlies W 10-6	Home – 5:30 p.m.
Sat. April 21	Tides (DH) W 8-7	Home – 11:00 a.m.
Tues. April 24	Bisons W 3-0	Away – 5:30 p.m.
Sat. April 28	Zephyrs (DH) L 6-1	Away – noon

The team is doing fine...no thanks to me.
I open my laptop and pull up the Ravens

website. When I click on statistics, a row of
names and numbers appears on the screen.

Player	Abs	R	H	RBI	BA
M. Jones	27	8	14	7	.519
J. Clark	26	6	8	4	.308
P. Rodriguez	26	3	9	5	.346
C. McLaughlin	25	3	10	4	.400
J. Bertelli	23	4	9	3	.391
W. Draves	22	4	7	2	.318
A. Kim	20	3	6	2	.300
M. Long	17	3	5	3	.294
T. Thompson	14	2	4	1	.286
D. Diaz	10	1	2	1	.200
A. Hansen	8	1	3	1	.375
C. Kelly	7	1	2	1	.286
J. Walker	5	0	1	0	.200
N. Washington	4	0	0	0	.000

Abs = At-Bats   RBI = Runs Batted In
R = Runs scored   BA = Batting Average
H = Hits

"Four for fourteen," I mutter to myself.
That means I'm just two for twelve since

I lost my lucky sea glass. The Easton bat hasn't helped much either. Or touching the four corners of the plate or stepping over the baseline. I'm totally off my game. I've even booted a couple of plays in the field.

I haven't heard a thing from Mr. Kiley. I guess my lucky charm is gone for good.

I grab the mug full of sea glass and beach rocks from the top of the dresser and spill them onto my bedspread. I sort through the pile and pick out some of the best-looking pieces. I rub my thumb along the surfaces, hoping one will at least feel like my old blue one.

"Hurry up, Trey!" Mom shouts from the living room. "Cole and his dad will be here in a few minutes."

"Coming!" I yell back.

I close my eyes, thinking that something might draw me to a lucky one. I reach down and select a piece of sea glass and open my eyes. The smooth surface is dark brown, and it feels pretty good in my hand. I look over at the picture of my grandma and wonder what she would say about this one. It's got some sparkle and feels right. I bet she'd like it. Might even say it's lucky. I slip it in my baseball pants pocket and head downstairs.

Maybe I'll have better luck this game.

*****

I cup my hands over my mouth and shout as loud as I can from the Ravens bench. "Come on, Malik, be a hitter! Small box. Make it be in there!"

We're ahead 2–1 in the top of the fifth inning. We have runners on second and third, and one out with Malik at the plate.

The Clippers right-hander slings a side-arm fastball. Malik lets it go by.

"Ball four!" calls the umpire. "Take your base."

The bases are loaded. Now everyone's off the bench and on their feet as Cole comes to bat.

I stand with my fingers gripping the wire mesh in front of the dugout. We need some runs or Coach may not let me play at all this game. He has been using me less and less because I'm in such a slump. I can't say I blame him.

"Come on, Cole! Be a sticker. Get one you can drive."

Cole works the count to three balls and one strike. The next pitch is right in there.

Crack!

Cole drills a line drive down the left-field line. I lean out to see if the ball stays fair.

The umpire signals with his right hand. *Fair ball!* Everyone is running hard as the ball bounces into the left-field corner.

One run...two runs score. *Thank you, Cole!*

Two more hits bring in two more runs. We're ahead 6–1. That should be enough of a lead to get me into the game.

I see Coach studying the scorebook at the end of the inning. He holds up his hands. "We're going to make some changes," he says.

The players on the bench quiet down. I hold my breath.

"Cameron, go to right field for Alex. Dylan...first base." He pauses and checks the book again.

"Trey, go in for Josh at third."

I grab my glove, jump over the baseline, and sprint to third, half-hoping that the ball doesn't come to me. I sure don't need another error.

Fortunately, the ball doesn't find me. Two strikeouts and a pop out to Malik and we have the bats in our hands again.

Coach Locke calls out, "Peter, Cameron, and Dylan bat first. And then Trey. Everybody hits. We need some more runs."

Two outs later I'm standing in the on-deck circle hoping that Dylan gets a hit and saves my ups. I take the brown sea glass out of my pocket and rub it against the barrel of my bat. It couldn't hurt. And who knows? Maybe it'll help.

Dylan raps a base hit up the middle and races to first. I step into the batter's box and touch the four corners of the plate with the tip of my Easton bat.

The first pitch is in the dirt and bounces away from the Clippers catcher. Dylan takes off for second base. He's safe by a mile.

I step out of the box and take a deep

breath. Now I have a chance to drive in a run.

The next pitch looks a little outside. The umpire doesn't think so.

"Strike one!"

The next pitch is down the middle and I'm ready.

Crack!

I hit the ball on the nose but right at the third baseman. I'm hardly out of the batter's box when it smacks into his glove. Now I'm four for fifteen.

As I take the field, I figure I won't get up to bat again. But I still have a chance to make a play in the field. Anything to break my bad-luck streak. Sure enough, near the end of the inning, a Clippers batter smashes a hard hopper to third. But the ball takes a wicked hop that bounces over my head and is scored as a hit.

I'm thankful it didn't hit me in the face and I'm glad we won, but I really wanted to make at least one good play.

Cole tries to buck me up after the game as we walk to his parents' car.

"That was a great swing in the sixth inning. You really scorched that ball," he says. "Looks like you're coming out of your slump."

"Still, it wasn't a hit," I say, feeling the weight of every out I've made during the last few games.

"You hit it hard. That's all you can do. The rest is luck."

I reach into my pocket and take out the brown sea glass. I toss it into the low bushes near the parking lot.

Cole's right. Luck *is* part of any game. Trouble is, I don't seem to have the good kind anymore.

CHAPTER 10

I get home a little early after Wednesday's baseball practice.

"Don't worry about setting the table tonight," Mom calls from her bedroom. "We're going out to dinner."

"On a school night?"

"Your uncle Dave just called. He's in town for a business conference tomorrow. He's taking us to Dominic's. So get yourself cleaned up and put on your khakis and a good blue shirt."

"Can I wear sneaks?"

"I don't know, Trey. I guess so." She doesn't sound thrilled about the sneakers.

I take a quick shower and put on my nice clothes. When Mom comes down the hallway, she stops and checks herself out in the mirror. She looks great—like she's going to a party or something. Red dress, high heels. Not like my mom at all.

As soon as we get to the restaurant, I see why she got all dressed up. Dominic's is definitely not Pizza Hut. There's a fancy menu on the front door. I've never heard of half the foods listed. We go in. The servers are dressed in the same black and white outfits. Everything is set up with white tablecloths, heavy silverware, and cloth napkins.

I'm glad I decided to wear my good shoes instead of my sneaks.

A pretty woman in a fancy black dress comes over and asks, "Excuse me, do you have a reservation?"

"It should be under my brother's name," Mom says. "Burns. David Burns."

The woman checks her list and leads us to a table near the back. Uncle Dave stands up when he sees us coming. He's ten years older than my mom. His hair is grayer than it was the last time we saw him. He looks real cool, like some guy in a magazine, in his dark blue suit and light blue tie. His black shoes are so polished the lights of the restaurant reflect off the tips of his toes.

I bet Uncle Dave goes to places like Dominic's all the time.

"Whoa! Check out my little sis," he says as he gives Mom a hug. "You look fabulous. You make me feel a hundred years old."

My mom is smiling big time.

"And what about you, Trey? You must be three inches taller than you were the last time I saw you." Uncle Dave sticks out his hand. "Put it there, buddy. Long time, no see." We shake and my uncle nods with approval. "Good strong grip. Must be all the ball you're playing."

A waiter appears with three menus and asks us if we'd like something to drink. Uncle Dave glances at his menu and orders a bottle of wine with what sounds like a French name. I sense my chance and ask for a Coke. Mom doesn't overrule me.

As soon as the waiter walks away, Mom and Uncle Dave start catching up. I start eating breadsticks.

My uncle's a financial manager, so it isn't long before they get to the subject of money. They talk about 401(k)s, 529s, and all the other accounts he helped Mom set up after the divorce. Stuff I don't understand.

I zone out and try to make sense of the menu. I figure out one thing right away—the food here is really expensive.

Finally, Uncle Dave looks over at me. "Sorry, Trey. We've been talking about nothing but money and ignoring you," he says with a smile. "I just want to be sure you guys are saving enough to send you to a good college when the time comes. Although I hear there might be a baseball scholarship in your future. Your mom mentioned that you made some kind of special team this season."

"Yeah, I'm playing for the Ravens. It's a travel team."

The waiter brings over the menus and the bottle of wine Uncle Dave ordered and pours two glasses: one for my uncle and one for my mom. He places a glass full of ice in front of me and pours my Coke. My uncle takes a long taste of his wine, then loosens his tie with his left hand.

"So how's this new team going?"

"Okay, I guess."

"You don't sound too sure," Uncle Dave says.

"Yeah, well...I've been in kind of a hitting slump lately," I tell him. "I got two hits the first game, but only two more since then."

"Striking out a lot?" Uncle Dave asks.

"It's not that. I just haven't been getting hits." Then I add, "Not been very lucky, I guess."

"Luck," Uncle Dave says, "is when preparation..." He pauses and looks at Mom.

"...meets opportunity," she says, filling in the blank.

They laugh like it's some kind of old joke. But I don't see what's so hilarious.

"Or remember this one?" Mom makes her voice sound super serious. "You make your *own* luck."

Uncle Dave nods. "Or how about my favorite? 'The harder you work the luckier you get.'"

"You used to say those things?" I ask my mom.

"Not me." She smiles. "Your grandmother."

"I know Grandma had a million old sayings," I say. "But I don't remember those."

"I'll bet you can recite the sign from her house that we have hanging in our kitchen," Mom says.

"Sure. 'If you are lucky enough to live near the sea, you are lucky enough.'" I look at Mom and then at Uncle Dave. These new sayings don't match up with my memory of my grandmother. "I know Grandma believed in hard work and all that, but doesn't the sign in the kitchen mean she believed in luck, too?" I can't help thinking about my missing blue sea glass.

My mom considers my question for a moment as she swirls the wine in her glass. "Not really. Your grandmother believed all of us have talent, but that we all have to work hard to develop that talent. I never heard her say that luck had anything to do with succeeding at something."

Mom smiles as if she's remembering Grandma. "She could be pretty tough, you know. Remember, she was a fifth-grade teacher and then she became an elementary school principal. She retired just before you were born."

"Oh, she definitely believed in hard work," Uncle Dave says. "When your grandmother put up that sign you guys have in your house, she was probably thinking of a different kind of luck. You know, like when you say 'I'm so lucky to live by the beach,' you really mean 'I'm so grateful that I am able to live by the beach.' She always appreciated what she had worked hard for...like her beach house."

He takes another sip of wine. "My guess is you could put a lot of things on that sign she was grateful for. Like having kids...and grandkids."

I think about all those times I walked along the beach with Grandma. I knew she'd been a teacher. She was always pointing things out: starfish, barnacles, crabs. When the sun went down she would show me the stars in the night sky. She was always talking, always teaching.

"You knew your grandmother when she was older," Uncle Dave explains. "You were the youngest grandchild. She had mellowed a lot by then." Then he lowers his voice as if he is telling me a secret. "And I always thought you were her favorite."

The waiter arrives. "Are you ready to order?"

"I'll have the halibut," Mom says and snaps her menu shut.

It's my turn. "Um...I don't know," I mumble. All the choices seem strange.

"Do you like steak?" Uncle Dave asks.

"Sure."

"He'll have the Chateaubriand, medium rare."

"When I saw that on the menu, I was afraid it might be roasted brains or something," I say, feeling a little embarrassed.

Mom laughs. "We don't have Chateaubriand very often."

"Then it will be a special treat." Uncle

Dave smiles and then orders something called Sea Bass Florentine.

"Now back to baseball," he says as he hands his menu to the waiter. "Your luck will even out over the course of the year. You'll get your share of hits if you keep working at it. That's the important thing."

"Maybe," I say. Uncle Dave may know about money, but I'm not sure he knows a lot about baseball.

"Keep grinding away," Uncle Dave continues. "Sometimes the line drives get caught and the dribblers turn into hits."

Dinner arrives. The food is arranged on the plate like little paintings.

I cut into the meat. It's pink in the middle and tastes fantastic.

"How's that steak?" Uncle Dave asks.

"Great."

Sitting in Dominic's in my good shoes, eating my Chateaubriand and halfway listening to Uncle Dave and Mom talk, I start to think back on what they said about Grandma and what she thought about hard work and luck.

Seems like I had it all wrong. Grandma didn't think much about luck after all.

Then I wonder what Grandma would think about lucky bats or touching the corners of the plate and not stepping on the baselines.

And me still hoping that Mr. Kiley finds my lucky sea glass.

CHAPTER 11

The apartment is quiet. It's after school on Thursday. There's no baseball practice and I don't have much homework.

"Anybody home?"

No answer.

I walk into the kitchen and see a note on the counter.

2:05 pm
Trey—

Have a meeting this PM. Be home @ 7.
Pls set table for dinner. Beautiful day—no TV!
Go to park and do something!

Love you,
Mom

I smile. I have one of those moms who thinks watching television is some kind of crime. And don't even mention video games. She won't let them in the apartment. I'm not really surprised about that, though. A lot of video games are kind of stupid.

I text Cole to see if he wants to hang out. No luck. He says he has to go to a dentist appointment.

I throw on some gym shorts and by 3:30 I'm jogging to Crocker Field. Maybe I can play some hoops or get into a game of pickup soccer.

I cut down a side street. Less traffic. I see some kids playing basketball in the street. Too young. Probably fourth or fifth graders. I keep walking.

I turn on to Main Street and walk past the stores and a vacant lot or two. Before long I'm at the edge of Crocker Field. I'm surprised there aren't many kids in the park on such a sunny day. They're probably sitting at home staring at a video game.

A few high school boys are shooting hoops on one of the courts. This game looks a little too fast and serious for me. Two other kids are passing a lacrosse ball back and forth inside the empty tennis courts. I'm not a lacrosse guy.

On the far side of the field, I spot a man sitting on a bucket and throwing soft toss to someone who looks about my age. The boy is hitting the balls into a chain-link backstop. I start walking in that direction, figuring maybe they'll give me a few swings.

Even from far away I can tell that the kid with the bat is pretty good. He's got a powerful swing that sends every ball into the backstop with a loud *clank*. As I get closer I see that the guy sitting on the bucket has on a shirt and tie. Then I recognize the batter.

"Hey, Malik. I thought we didn't have practice today."

Malik looks up for a second. "Hey, Trey." Then he takes his swing. *Clank!* "You can always use more practice."

"Why? You're already the best kid on the team."

"Thanks, but I want to get better."

His answer makes me think about my

grandmother and her "good, better, best" thing.

He smacks three straight line drives into the backstop. *Clank! Clank! Clank!*

He points the bat at the guy sitting on the bucket. "By the way, this is my dad. Dad, this is Trey."

"Hi, Mr. Jones."

"Yeah, I know who Trey is." Mr. Jones smiles and holds up a battered baseball. "You've done a nice job backing up at second and third."

I don't much like the sound of "backing up," but I guess he means it as a compliment.

"You want to take a few swings?" Malik asks.

I eye the bat he's holding out. It isn't my favorite Easton. "Um, I don't know..."

"Aw, come on. Give it a try."

I take the bat and slam a few into the backstop, but none of my hits are as power-packed as Malik's line drives. Malik and I take turns with the bat until his father's phone starts buzzing. He takes it out of his pocket and stares at the screen.

"We've gotta go, Malik. Your mother wants us home ASAP."

Malik and I pick up the baseballs and put them in the bucket. Mr. Jones slings his suit jacket over his shoulder and they walk off together.

"See you at practice," Malik calls back.

"Okay. See you tomorrow."

I stand near the backstop and watch them walk away. Malik and his dad talk back and forth like they're best friends or something. After they're out of sight, I decide to head back to our apartment.

Malik's lucky to have a dad to throw him soft toss. No wonder he's so good. He's got someone to practice with.

CHAPTER 12

"You're early," Coach Locke says. He's right. The Ravens practice won't start for at least another half hour.

I showed up early for a good reason. I've been thinking since I saw Malik practicing with his dad. And I've been thinking about the saying Uncle Dave said my grandmother liked best: *You make your own luck.*

"I need some extra batting practice," I tell the coach. "I was hoping somebody could pitch to me, do some soft toss, or maybe I could just practice hitting off a tee."

"Good idea," Coach Locke agreed. "You've been struggling a bit the past couple of weeks. You're not going to get better by just showing up for practice. You need more swings than that." He points toward the batting cage. "Why don't I throw you a few pitches?"

I reach for my Easton bat and then think again. That bat hasn't had many hits in it lately. I grab a Louisville Slugger instead and go into the cage. Coach Locke stands at the plate across from me. "First, let's go over some fundamentals," he says. "The best way to break out of a slump is to go back to basics."

He reels off a list of tips:

Find a good balanced stance. It all starts with the legs.

Keep your hands back in a ready position.

Get your front foot down...fast.

Rip the bat across the plate.

Use your best bat speed. Swing like you mean it.

Coach steps behind the L-shaped screen. "Ready?" he asks.

I nod and take a good balanced stance with my hands back. I'm ready.

The pitches come in fast and furious. At first, I get weak contact and a bunch of fouls, pretty much the way I've been hitting—or not hitting—lately. But one by one, I concentrate on Coach's other tips. I begin to get my foot down faster and get more contact. After a while, I feel like I'm increasing my bat speed. Not Malik kind of swings, but I'm definitely improving.

Coach Locke fires me another fastball. "Get that foot down quicker!"

Before the next pitch he yells, "Have your bat ready! Drive it back through the middle!"

By the time the other Ravens show up for practice, I'm sweating like crazy. But I'm swinging better and feeling more confident.

"Good workout," Coach Locke says as we walk out of the cage. "Your swing is really coming along. Why don't you get here early for the next practice and I'll throw to you again?"

"Sure, thanks."

In spite of my warm-up with Coach Locke, practice is the same old story. Most of the time I'm stuck in back of Mason at second and Josh at third. When we scrimmage, I get a hit and a couple of chances in the field. But

I don't get a fraction of the swings I got in my pre-practice workout.

Coach Locke is right. Just coming to practice isn't enough. If I want to get better, I'm going to have to work at it more. Like Malik.

After practice I ask Coach Locke if he could stay a few minutes and hit me some extra grounders.

He shakes his head. "Sorry, Trey. Maybe another time. Today I have to pick up my daughter Jennifer at her dance class—that's her sport."

"That's okay," I say, turning to go.

"Hey, Trey!" Malik calls. "You want me to hit you some grounders?"

"Sure."

Malik drops his glove on the grass and grabs a bat.

I run out to third base. "Where should I throw the ball?" I ask. "We don't have anybody at first base."

"Toss it back here," he says, motioning to the area around home plate. "I'll try to catch it or hit it back to you."

The first hit is a high hopper. I step in and

take it around my waist. I soft-toss it back. Five or six hits later, Malik starts handing out fielding advice. He sounds just like Coach Locke.

"Get up on the balls of your feet. Ready position. Remember your footwork."

I keep that in mind as I field the next grounder.

It works. I *am* getting a little better.

"Get in front!" Malik shouts when he hits another hopper toward me. "Attack the ball!"

"Need a first baseman?" Mr. Kiley lays down his rake and ambles over to the bag in his jeans and work shirt.

"Sure."

Mr. Kiley motions to Malik. "Throw me your glove."

Malik tosses him his mitt. Mr. Kiley puts it on, punches the pocket, and gets into position next to the bag.

I range to my left to snag the next grounder and toss a rainbow throw over to Mr. Kiley.

"Come on!" he says in a sharp voice. "You got a better arm than that. Fire it over. Right in the chest. Don't worry, you won't hurt me."

I bobble the next grounder but recover. I throw low and hard to first. Mr. Kiley stretches out and snaps the one-hopper off the dirt like a pro.

"He's out!" He signals with his right hand. "Good play."

We keep going until a film of sweat covers my arms. Grounder after grounder. Throw after throw. Mr. Kiley picks it at first base like a Gold Glove winner. Finally, he holds up his hands. "I better get back to work," he says and tosses the glove to Malik.

"Thanks!" I shout. "Hey, you're pretty good."

Mr. Kiley smiles. "I played a bit...back in the old days." He waves and heads over toward his rake.

"I guess that's enough...for today," I say.

Malik and I walk away from the field. "I didn't know Mr. Kiley could play ball like that," he says. "He's pretty slick with the leather."

I nod. "Yeah, that old guy is just full of surprises."

CHAPTER 13

I lean back on the bench. "Doesn't seem like all my extra work is paying off," I mutter to Cole. "I wonder if Coach Locke talked to Coach D?"

"Don't worry, you'll get in."

"When? It's the sixth inning."

"Coach will play you. He's seen how hard you've been working the last few days."

I lean over and stare at the dugout dirt. I'm not so sure.

"Trey, go in for Josh!" Coach Locke calls.

My head pops up and Cole gives me an I-told-you-so look. I trot out to the infield. Just as I start to step over the baseline, I stop. I kick the chalk instead.

I check the scoreboard.

INNING	1	2	3	4	5	6	7
Ravens	1	0	0	2	0	2	
Redbirds	1	1	0	1	0		

It's the bottom of the sixth and we're leading 5–3. If we stay ahead, I'll get to play one whole inning. Big deal. I probably won't even get an at-bat.

But I get some action in the field right away. The Redbirds batter smacks a hard hopper to third. All my fielding practice makes it easy. I scoop up the ball and fire a strike to first base. One out.

Two more outs and we're on the bench, looking to add to our lead. I walk over to Coach Locke.

"When am I up this inning?"

He turns over the scorebook and studies the list of names. "Let's see, Cole, Peter...ah, you're up fifth."

I can tell he sees the disappointment on my face. "Don't worry, Trey. They'll get some hits to save your ups. Just be ready when you're at the plate."

No such luck. We go down, one-two-three, and are back in the field in the bottom of the seventh (and last) inning. This time, I stomp on the foul line when I run out to third base.

The first Redbird strikes out and the second batter walks. Runner at first, one out.

A sharp grounder streaks to my left. I'm up on the balls of my feet and dive out, knocking the ball down. I grab the ball, pop to my feet, and look to second base. No chance. So I throw to first, getting the runner by half a step.

Two outs, runner on second. The Redbirds are down to their last out. The batter works the count to three balls, two strikes. Now they're down to their last strike.

The infield fills with chatter. Our team can almost taste another win.

"Come on, close the door!"

"No free passes."

"Make him a hitter!"

Our closer, Noah Washington, winds up and tries to get a little something extra on his fastball.

The batter swings. *Wham!*

The ball rockets out to left field. I know it's trouble. I turn and see Cole racing back to the wall. Back...back...until he has nowhere to go. Cole looks up helplessly as the ball sails over the fence.

Home run! The game is tied 5–5.

Secretly, I'm kind of excited as I watch the Redbirds batter circle the bases. I know I'm not supposed to root against my own team, but this means I'll get to hit in the bottom of the inning.

We race in after a pop fly is the third out.

"Alex, Trey, and Dylan!" Coach D calls out. "Let's get a run and win it right here."

Alex grounds out. There's one out and nobody on when I step into the batter's box. I'm about to touch the four corners of the plate but decide against it. What did Grandma say? 'Luck is when preparation meets opportunity.' All my practice with Coach Locke has made me prepared and here is my opportunity.

I let a ball and a strike go by. The third pitch is a fastball and I'm ready.

Whack!

It's a line drive heading for the gap in left-center field. When I take off from the batter's box, I'm thinking extra bases. I look out to left field as I approach first base and see the Redbirds left fielder leaping up and tumbling on the outfield grass. He bolts to his feet holding the ball in his glove. What a catch!

I don't believe it. I rip my batting helmet off my head. I feel like smashing it against something, but I force myself to set it down on the bench.

"Good swing," Cole says. "You hit it right on the nose. Nothing you could do. That kid just made a great play on you."

We can't score in the bottom of the seventh inning, so we keep playing...and playing...and playing.

Extra innings are fine with me. I get

a line-drive hit in the ninth inning and a "seeing-eye" single in the twelfth that somehow bounces between the shortstop and third baseman. Like Uncle Dave said, sometimes the dribblers get through. I also make a couple of plays at third.

I'm having a blast. Some of the players and parents are getting tired, but I wouldn't mind if the game went on forever. At least I'm getting to play.

The Redbirds score in the top of the fourteenth inning when they turn two walks and a double into two runs. We're down 7–5 when we return to the dugout.

"Got to get them back!" Coach D calls out. But I'm not sure the guys who have played all fourteen innings even care about coming back.

"Got to get three runs," Malik says as he marches up and down the bench clapping his hands. Then he adds with a sly smile, "Not two runs, understand? *Three!* Let's end it here."

We squeeze a walk and a single between a strikeout and a fly-out to spark some hope.

There are runners on first and second with two outs when I step to the plate.

Again I'm tempted to touch the four corners of the plate, but I hold back.

I foul off a couple of pitches and then let a high fastball and a changeup in the dirt go by. Two balls, two strikes, two runners on. We need at least two runs.

A belt-high fastball spins in. It looks a little outside so I hold back.

"Strike three!" The home plate umpire calls. "You're out!"

No way that was a strike. "That was outside!" I shout. The umpire takes off his mask and turns away. The game is over.

After the tired teams shake hands, Coach Locke comes up and pats me on the shoulder.

"Don't feel bad, Trey. I think the umpire just wanted to go home. I thought that last pitch was outside too. But with two strikes, you've got to swing at anything close."

For some weird reason, I don't feel bad. Even though I struck out to end the game, I'm happier than I've been in weeks. I actually played a whole game—more than seven innings. Got a couple of hits and made a few plays in the field.

"Good game," Cole says as we walk away from the field. "You were lucky the game went into extra innings."

I smile. I'm feeling great, and I know it doesn't have anything to do with luck.

CHAPTER 14

Don't forget to put your dishes in the dishwasher, boys," Cole's mother says.

"Thanks a lot for the dinner, Mrs. McLaughlin." I slip my plate into the rack. "The chicken was great."

"Don't thank me," she says, laughing. "Mr. McLaughlin picked it up at the Fresh Fields take-out counter."

"I'm a great cook," Cole's dad says with a wink. "I can pick up anything you want from the store." He looks at his wife. "When is Trey's mom picking him up?"

"Eight o'clock. She has a late meeting."

"All right, then. You guys have time to get some homework done," Mr. McLaughlin says, clapping his hands like a coach. "You got that history test tomorrow, right? Better run on up to Cole's room and get some studying done."

Cole and I start upstairs.

"Remember," his dad calls after us. "I want you guys studying. Not playing on the computer."

I've always liked Cole's room. It's big and filled with sports posters, trophies, and souvenirs from all the games he and his father have attended over the years.

"Why don't we test each other on stuff in the study packets?" I suggest.

"Okay, you ask first."

I look over the questions. "Who was Franklin Delano Roosevelt's vice-presidential running mate in the 1944 election?"

"Come on, start me with an easier one."

"What do you mean? That *is* an easy one. He became president in 1945 after Roosevelt died."

"Oh yeah, Harry S. Truman."

"You get extra credit if you can tell me what the *S* stands for," I say with a grin.

"That's not in the study packet...is it?"

"I know, but try to guess."

"I have no idea."

"Nothing."

"What?"

"Nothing. Truman said his middle name was just a letter."

Cole tosses a pillow at me. "Ask me a real question."

"Okay, name the place where Churchill, Roosevelt, and Stalin met for the last time during World War II."

"Yalta."

"Where is it?"

"That's not in the packet."

"But don't you want to know?" I ask.

"Not if it's not going to be on Ms. Ko's test."

I can't help showing off. "Yalta is a resort city in Crimea on the Black Sea," I said. I toss the study packet to Cole. "Why don't you give me a chance now?" I ask, feeling super confident.

Sure enough, I get six answers in a row right. I knock them right out of the park. No problem.

"Man, you are on a hot streak," Cole says.

"I've been studying." It's true. I've been keeping up with the reading and paying more attention in class. I figure that studying is like practicing; going over a fact again and again makes it a lot easier to remember on a test. History is getting to be my favorite subject. It's like a super-cool puzzle about how everything in the past fits together.

"You've been playing better, too," Cole adds. "What are you hitting these days?"

"Seven hits for my last fifteen times at bat. So I'm eleven out of thirty overall—that comes out to .367."

"No way. That's like Ty Cobb's batting average."

"No really," I insist. "My average has been getting better ever since I started taking extra batting every practice with Coach Locke."

"I want to check our statistics," Cole says, grabbing his laptop.

"Your dad doesn't want us on the computer, remember? He thinks we're studying."

"My dad doesn't want us *playing games* on

the computer," Cole says. "We're not playing, we're doing research. Anyway, this will only take a minute."

Cole's fingers tap across the keys. "Let's see…" I look over Cole's shoulder even though I know exactly what he is going to find.

Player	Abs	R	H	RBI	BA
M. Jones	76	18	37	17	.487
J. Clark	72	15	21	9	.292
P. Rodriguez	70	9	24	14	.343
C. McLaughlin	69	12	26	12	.377
W. Draves	66	11	20	7	.303
A. Kim	62	10	21	7	.339
J. Bertelli	59	11	17	8	.288
M. Long	44	6	12	5	.273
T. Thompson	30	5	11	4	.367
A. Hansen	24	3	7	3	.292
D. Diaz	22	2	5	2	.227
C. Kelly	18	1	4	1	.222
J. Walker	13	0	2	1	.154
N. Washington	12	0	1	0	.083

Abs = At-Bats
R = Runs scored
H = Hits

RBI = Runs Batted In
BA = Batting Average

"Man, you *are* hitting .367," Cole says in disbelief. "Seven for your last fifteen. You're getting to be a tough out."

"I told you. Me and Ty Cobb."

"You got a new lucky piece of sea glass or something?" Cole asks.

I shake my head. "No. I'm just practicing more."

"I saw that you switched to a new bat."

"I know, but the bat doesn't have anything to do with it."

"You still jumping over the baseline?"

I can feel my face getting warm. I didn't realize that Cole had noticed *all* my lucky rituals. I shake my head again, harder this time.

"No, it's none of that stuff." I point at the screen. "Hey, take a look...I'm even catching up to you."

Cole makes a face. "Are you kidding me? I got a lot more at-bats than you."

"Come on, don't rub it in." I look back to the screen. "Do you think Coach D will ever play me more?"

"He *is* playing you more. Maybe he'll put you in early against the Zephyrs. They're really tough."

Cole's right about Coach D. Since I started practicing, he has put me in sooner, usually during the fourth inning instead of waiting until the fifth or sixth inning. But I still want to stay in the games longer...or even better, be a starter.

"I thought we were supposed to be studying," I say, changing the subject.

Cole grabs the study questions again. "Name the two Japanese cities the United States bombed with nuclear weapons."

"Hiroshima and Nagasaki."

"Who was the Japanese Emperor at the end of World War II?"

"Hirohito."

"What claim did Hirohito have to give up following the war?"

"The claim that he ruled over Japan by divine power."

"Give me a break!" Cole blurts out. "You already know all the answers! You're like

Veronica Valdez or something."

I raise my arms in triumph as if I had just hit a walk-off home run. "Like you said, I'm getting to be a tough out."

CHAPTER 15

At the top of the third inning, Coach D shouts, "Trey, go in for Mason at second base!"

I have to admit, I'm surprised. Happy, but surprised. Maybe he's sending me in because we're trailing the Zephyrs 4–1. Our team seems flat. The Zephyrs are good, but we look like we've been standing out in the hot sun too long. Maybe Coach is trying to shake things up. Fine with me. I'll give it my best shot.

After a one-two-three top of the third inning, we run back into the dugout.

"Jayden, Josh, and Malik!" Coach D shouts. "Top of the order. Let's go, we need some runs."

I walk over to Coach Locke and ask him when I'll be up this inning.

Coach checks the scorebook. "Sixth. Be ready. Their pitcher's pretty good. He throws hard, so get your hands moving."

I sit down on the bench next to Cole.

"I told you these guys are tough," he says.

Malik walks by with a bat in his hand. "We can beat them," he calls back over his shoulder.

I stay quiet. There's a lot of the game left. I feel a little nervous. My mom's here and I'm not used to coming in to play so early. Part of me still wishes I had my lucky blue sea glass. I know it probably wouldn't help. But still…it couldn't hurt. Could it?

The Ravens start a small rally with a walk and a hit. But Cole strikes out to end the inning. We're still down 4–1 after three innings. I'll be leading off in the bottom of the fourth.

The Zephyrs threaten in the top of the inning. They have runners on first and third with two outs. We can't let them score any more runs or we'll be too far behind to come back. The whole team senses it. The infield chatter gets louder.

"Tighten up. Got to make a play!"

"One more out. Bear down."

"Two in the box. Let's get the third!"

Crack!

A sharp grounder burns along the grass to my right. I scramble over and backhand the ball. With all my momentum going toward second base, I don't have a chance to get the runner at first so I flip a desperate off-balanced throw to second.

Malik is there. He grabs the ball bare-handed and touches the bag.

Got him! We're out of the inning.

"Great play!" yells Cole. "Way to go, Trey!"

It's weird how in baseball it always seems that the guy who makes the great play in the field is the one who leads off the next inning. This time I'm that guy.

"Stay hot, man," Peter Rodriguez says to me standing near the on-deck circle. "Remember to touch all four sides of the plate."

I grab a bat and dig into the batter's box.

But I don't take Peter's advice. No touching the four corners of home plate, no nothing.

A fastball blisters the outside corner. *Strike one!*

I lay off a high one but can't catch up with an inside fastball. I'm behind in the count now. One ball, two strikes. I choke up on the bat a bit and remind myself to shorten my swing. Put it in play and just meet it.

I foul off two pitches.

The next pitch is way outside. The count is even. Two balls, two strikes. My Raven teammates are up and shouting.

"Good sticker!"

"Way to battle!"

"Just takes one!"

A fastball spins in toward the outside corner of the plate. It's too close to take with two strikes, so I swing.

Smack!

The ball slices over the first baseman's head and lands just inside the foul line. Fair ball! I round first base and take off for second, sliding in safely before the throw.

My leadoff double sparks a mini rally. A sacrifice bunt sends me to third and a grounder to shortstop gets me home. We got one back. It's 4–2 and we're in the game again.

We get another run in the fifth inning when Malik and Cole pound out a pair of doubles. The Zephyrs shortstop nails Cole with a perfect relay throw as he tries to stretch his hit into a triple. It's now 4–3 and I'm coming to bat with nobody on and two out.

I battle hard, fouling off three pitches and working the count to three balls and two strikes. A fastball buzzes inside. I hold back.

"Ball four. Take your base."

I look across the diamond to Coach D in the third-base coach's box. He wipes his hand across his chest and down his sleeve, and then he touches the tip of his cap. He wants me to steal on the first pitch.

As soon as the ball leaves the pitcher's hand, I take off running as if wild dogs are chasing me. The ball beats me to the bag but skips on the infield dirt and off the shortstop's glove.

Safe!

I race to home on a single by Alex to tie the score at 4–4. But we can't manage another run in the fifth inning.

Neither team scores in the sixth inning, so the game is still knotted up 4–4 going into the seventh and final inning.

"Come on, Ravens!" I yell as I run out to second base. "Let's win this thing."

CHAPTER 16

The Zephyrs squeeze a run out in the top of the seventh with a pair of singles and a sacrifice bunt. We're trailing 5–4 when we come to bat in the bottom of the inning.

Coach D is standing at the edge of the dugout. "Last licks!" he shouts. "Need some hits! Malik, Peter, Cole, and Trey. Everybody hits."

He points to the mound. "New pitcher. Take a look at him."

Malik, Cole, and I stand in the on-deck circle watching the Zephyrs closer warm up. Each pitch smacks into the catcher's glove.

"He throws hard," Cole says. "Harder than the other guy."

"Looks like everything's a fastball," Malik says. "Just get the bat going."

Malik gets things off to a good start with a single right up the middle. Peter flies out to left. Cole can't catch up with a fastball and pops up to the second baseman. Two outs and a runner on first. I step to the plate.

I'll admit it, I'm nervous. Maybe more excited than nervous. But I feel ready. I've been practicing and I'm hitting well. Still, I can't get the thought of my lucky sea glass out of my head. Maybe it would help. I shake the thought off and raise my bat.

Again, I get into a real battle, fouling off pitches and working the count. It's two balls, two strikes when I slap a hard grounder past the third baseman. The Zephyrs shortstop makes a great backhanded stab, spins, and throws hard to first. I'm running flat out. My foot hits the bag just before the ball reaches the first baseman's glove.

Safe!

"Good job, Trey!" Coach Locke slaps me

on the back. "Way to keep the line moving! There are two outs, so run on anything."

We've got a chance. Alex Kim is at the plate and he's a hot hitter. "Come on, Alex!" I shout. "Pick one you like!"

Alex tags a long fly to center field and I take off, racing hard. Maybe I can make it all the way home with the winning run. But the Zephyrs center fielder races back and reaches up, snapping the ball out of the air.

The third out. The inning is over. No comeback. We lose 5–4.

I jog to a stop and look up hopelessly into the late afternoon sky as the Zephyrs celebrate. After all that effort, I'm really disappointed that we didn't pull it out. Still, I'm happy about how I played in the game. Two hits, a walk, a big play in the field. I feel like I'm back.

Or maybe I'm just getting started.

Coach D calls us all over to the bench. "Nice game, guys. We played well. The Zephyrs are a very good team. Maybe the best in the league." He shrugs his shoulders as if to say 'that's baseball.' "But we've still got some games left. We'll get them next time. See you Tuesday. Be ready to practice hard."

I grab my stuff off the bench and glance over at the stands. Mom waves. I'm glad she was able to make the game. She didn't get to see us win, but at least she got to see me play a lot.

"Hey, Thompson!"

I turn around. Mr. Kiley's standing near the Zephyrs dugout. He's waving me over.

'Come over here."

"Wonder what he wants," Cole says.

"There's only one way to find out." I jog over.

Mr. Kiley smiles through his scraggly beard. "I think I got something here you might be interested in." He digs into the right front pocket of his jeans and pulls something out. I spy a flash of blue in his hand.

"Where'd you find it?" I ask, staring wide-eyed at my sea glass.

"Over there. Along the third-base dugout," he says, tossing it to me. "I was doing some clipping and it caught my eye. I can see why you wanted it back. That's one good-looking lucky charm."

I turn the sea glass over in my fingers, feeling its smooth sides. "I can't believe you found it after all these weeks."

"Well…" A guilty look creeps across Mr. Kiley's face. "Actually I found it a couple of weeks after you told me about it."

"Well…why…?" I stammer. "I mean…."

He shrugs. "Any time I saw you, it seemed like you were busy practicing with Coach Locke or Malik." He pauses. "I didn't want to interrupt that."

I stare at the old man, trying to figure him out.

"Anyway," he continues, "it seemed like you were getting along fine without it. What are you hitting now?"

I think for a moment. I got two hits in my two at-bats today. That makes me thirteen for thirty-two on the season. I take out my phone and click on the calculator app.

"I'm hitting .406 for the season."

"Hold on for a minute. Did you say .406?"

he asks. "That's a pretty famous baseball number."

"What do you mean?"

"That was Ted Williams's batting average in 1941," Mr. Kiley says. "He was the last major leaguer to hit .400."

"Was Ted Williams superstitious?" I ask, remembering our conversation from weeks before.

Mr. Kiley shakes his head. "I don't think so. But I know he did practice a lot."

I flip the sea glass over in my hand. It shines like a bit of the blue ocean. "Thanks, Mr. Kiley. Thanks for everything."

CHAPTER 17

"Wash up and get ready for dinner," Mom says as we walk into the apartment. "I'll set the table."

"What are we having?"

"I got some hamburger."

"Not Chateaubriand?" I joke.

She smiles. "No, you'll have to wait until Uncle Dave comes back into town to have Chateaubriand again."

I toss my dirty uniform into the clothes hamper and put on my sweat pants and an old Lookouts T-shirt. Just then I remember Mr. Kiley and the sea glass. I reach back into the hamper and pull the chunk of glass from my uniform pants pocket. Feeling the smooth blue edges makes me think of my grandmother. I can almost hear her whispering, "I am so lucky to have you as a grandson."

I look at the mug that holds my collection of sea glass and stones. I can't put the blue sea glass back there. I don't need it for baseball or history tests anymore, but it's still special. I need to find another place. I look around my room. I see the spot.

I place the blue sea glass on the dresser in front of the picture of my grandmother and me.

We're at the beach in the photo. The sky's a clear blue. I'm about seven. My hair's wet and I'm so skinny I look like could blow away in a gust of sea breeze. Grandma is sitting low in a beach chair. Her hair is gray and her face is tanned. We're both smiling. She's holding me and I'm leaning into her.

The blue sea glass looks perfect with the picture.

I think about her sign that now hangs above our kitchen sink.

If you are lucky enough to live near the sea,
you are lucky enough.

We don't live near the sea.

My dad is way out in California and I hardly ever hear from him.

I've still got a long way to go before I'm as good at baseball as Malik or even Cole.

Still, I'm lucky. Not the touch-the-corner-of-home-plate or magic-sea-glass lucky.

But...

Lucky to be playing baseball with my friends on the Ravens.

Lucky to have my mom.

Lucky to have a coach like Mr. Locke to pitch me extra batting practice.

Lucky to have all my memories of my grandmother and our days at the beach.

Even lucky that Mr. Kiley waited a while to give me back my sea glass.

I guess you could say I'm lucky enough.

THE REAL STORY: BASEBALL SUPERSTITIONS

Baseball is full of superstitions.

Maybe it's because the game is so hard—think of trying to hit a 95-mile-per-hour fastball. Some players believe they need a little bit of help, or a little bit of luck, to be successful.

Luck is definitely part of the game. Sometimes a lazy pop-up finds a spot in the outfield for a hit while a crushed line drive ends up in a fielder's glove. In the major leagues, if a player gets just one more hit a week, that could be the difference between being a .250 hitter and a .300 hitter. In other words, one lucky hit a week could be the difference between being an average player and an All-Star.

Players have believed in superstitions and jinxes from the earliest days of baseball.

Honus Wagner, the Hall of Fame shortstop for the Pittsburgh Pirates from 1900 to 1917, believed that a bat only had so many hits in it. He would stop using a bat after a hundred hits. Still, "The Flying Dutchman," as Wagner was called, used plenty of bats. He had 3,420 hits during his career.

Willie Stargell, another Pittsburgh Hall of Famer who played from 1962 to 1982, would not use a Willie Stargell model bat. He thought it was bad luck. Stargell only swung bats with other people's names on them. This superstition worked well for him. Stargell blasted 475 home runs during his 21-year career.

As Mr. Kiley said, Wade Boggs (who played from 1982 to 1999) ate chicken before every ball game. But this Hall of Fame third baseman had lots of other superstitions.

For example, Boggs started his batting practice at the exact same time before every night game—5:17 p.m. He also took 150 grounders, no more and no less, for fielding practice during warm-ups. Finally, the twelve-time All-Star and five-time batting champion wrote the Hebrew word *chai,* which means "life," in the batter's box every time he came to the plate. Just like Trey, lots of players are superstitious about stepping on the foul lines when they come on and off the field. One such player was New York Yankee pitcher and later pitching coach, Mel Stottlemyre (1964 to 1974). He never stepped on the foul line until one day when he absentmindedly stepped on the line before a game with the Minnesota Twins.

Here's what happened. The first batter smashed a ball right off Stottlemyre's left leg for a hit. The next four Twins batters got hits, including three extra-base hits, and the Twins scored five runs in the first inning.

"I haven't stepped on a foul line since," Stottlemyre, said recalling the game.

There are lots of superstitions concerning clothes. One is not to change clothes during a winning streak or hitting streak.

Tony LaRussa, manager of the St. Louis Cardinals, had a "lucky" warm-up jacket. Detroit Tigers manager, Jim Leyland, wore the same pair of boxers (unwashed!) during any Tiger winning streak.

Pitcher Tim Lincecum (2007 to 2016) had a lot of success early in his career, including two Cy Young awards as the outstanding pitcher in the National League in 2008 and 2009. Maybe Lincecum was so good because he wore the same hat during his nine years with the San Francisco Giants. That's right, one hat for nine years.

Relief pitcher John Wetteland did something similar. Wetteland wore one hat—no matter how dirty or sweat-stained it got—for each of his major league seasons.

Craig Biggio (1988 to 2007), who was selected to the Hall of Fame after playing twenty seasons with the Houston Astros, wore a batting helmet that was covered in pine tar. So did Vladimir Guerrero (1996 to 2011).

There must be something lucky about pine tar on a batting helmet. Biggio knocked out 3,060 hits during his career while Guerrero smacked 2,590 career hits.

Another baseball superstition is not to talk to a pitcher who is throwing a no-hitter or even mention that he is throwing a no-hitter. Players and announcers are afraid they will "jinx" the pitcher.

Probably the most famous no-hitter was when New York Yankee hurler, Don Larsen, threw a no-hitter (in fact, a perfect game— twenty-seven straight outs) against the Brooklyn Dodgers in the 1956 World Series.

The Yankees radio announcer, Mel Allen, wanted to tell his listeners that Larsen was making baseball history by throwing a no-hitter in a World Series game but didn't want to jinx the Yankee starter. So Allen simply mentioned at some point "the Yankees have all the hits in the game."

Another announcer, Lindsay Nelson, didn't worry about telling his listeners about a no-hitter. Nelson said, "I figure, if anything I say in the broadcasting booth can influence anything going on down on the field, I ought to be getting more money."

So, do all these superstitions work? Maybe they do in a way, if they help a player to relax and focus on the game. But it's important to remember that all the players mentioned above—Wagner, Boggs, Biggio, and the rest—worked hard to reach the major leagues and become the players they were. They didn't just depend on rituals and lucky hats.

My guess is they knew, as Trey found out, that practice works a lot better than any lucky bat or superstition.

Or even a bit of blue sea glass.

ACKNOWLEDGMENTS

Thanks to my son, Liam Bowen,
who is the Associate Head Baseball
Coach at University of Maryland–Baltimore
County (UMBC). He helped me with some
of the technical aspects of the baseball
advice given in the story.

Thanks to my brother Pete and his wife Sandy,
who have a sign in their home in Marblehead
bearing the following message:

*If you are lucky enough to live near the sea, you
are lucky enough.*

That sign got me thinking about this story.

SOURCES

The information concerning the baseball superstitions in "The Real Story" came from several sources. They include these books and articles:

Baseball's Greatest Quotations by Paul Dickson (Harper Perennial, 1991)

I'm Fascinated by Sacrifice Flies: Inside the Game We All Love by Tim Kurkjian (St. Martin's Press, 2016)

"Baseball's 50 Weirdest All-Time Superstitions" by Robert Knapel (*Bleacher Report*, May 11, 2012)

"Baseball Hoodoos, Superstitions and Rituals" by Paul Dickson (Society for American Baseball Research, November 23, 2015)

ABOUT THE AUTHOR

Fred Bowen was a Little Leaguer who loved to read. Now he is the author of many action-packed books of sports fiction. He has also written a weekly sports column for kids in the *Washington Post* since 2000.

Fred played lots of sports growing up, including soccer at Marblehead High School. For thirteen years, he coached kids' baseball, soccer, and basketball teams. Some of his stories spring directly from his coaching experience and his sports-happy childhood in Marblehead, Massachusetts.

Fred holds a degree in history from the University of Pennsylvania and a law degree from George Washington University. He was a lawyer for many years before retiring to become a full-time children's author. Bowen has been a guest author at schools and conferences across the country, as well as the

Smithsonian Institute in Washington, D. C., and The Baseball Hall of Fame.

Fred lives in Silver Spring, Maryland, with his wife Peggy Jackson. Their son is a college baseball coach, and their daughter is a reading teacher in Washington, D. C.

For more information check out the author's website at *www.fredbowen.com.*

HEY, SPORTS FANS!

Don't miss these action-packed books in the Fred Bowen Sports Story series!

 **BASEBALL**

Dugout Rivals
PB: $6.95 / 978-1-56145-515-7
Last year Jake was one of his team's best players. But this season it looks like a new kid is going to take Jake's place as team leader. Can Jake settle for second-best?

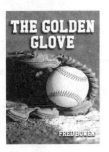

The Golden Glove
PB: $6.95 / 978-1-56145-505-8
Without his lucky glove, Jamie doesn't believe in his ability to lead his baseball team to victory. How will he learn that faith in oneself is the most important equipment for any game?

The Kid Coach
PB: $6.95 / 978-1-56145-506-5
Scott and his teammates can't find an adult to coach their team, so they must find a leader among themselves.

Perfect Game
PB: $6.95 / 978-1-56145-625-3
HC: $14.95 / 978-1-56145-701-4
Isaac is determined to pitch a perfect game. He gets close a couple of times, but when things go wrong he can't get his head back in the game. Then Isaac meets an interesting Unified Sports basketball player who shows him a whole new way to think about perfect.

Playoff Dreams
PB: $6.95 / 978-1-56145-507-2
Brendan is one of the best players in the league, but no matter how hard he tries, he can't make his team win.

T. J.'s Secret Pitch
PB: $6.95 / 978-1-56145-504-1
T. J.'s pitches just don't pack the power they need to strike out the batters, but the story of 1940s baseball hero Rip Sewell and his legendary eephus pitch may help him find a solution.

Throwing Heat
PB: $6.95 / 978-1-56145-540-9
HC: $14.95 / 978-1-56145-573-7
Jack throws the fastest pitches around, but lately his blazing fastballs haven't been enough. He's got to learn new pitches to stay ahead of the batters. But can he resist bringing the heat?

Winners Take All
PB: $6.95 / 978-1-56145-512-6
Kyle makes a poor decision to cheat in a big game. Someone discovers the truth and threatens to reveal it. What can Kyle do now?

BASKETBALL

The Final Cut
PB: $6.95 / 978-1-56145-510-2
Four friends realize that they may not all make the team and that the tryouts are a test—not only of their athletic skills, but also of their friendship.

Full Court Fever
PB: $6.95 / 978-1-56145-508-9
The Falcons have the skill but not the height to win their games. Will the full-court zone press be the solution to their problem?

Hardcourt Comeback
PB: $6.95 / 978-1-56145-516-4
Brett blew a key play in an important game. Now he feels like a loser for letting his teammates down—and he keeps making mistakes. How can Brett become a "winner" again?

Off the Rim
PB: $6.95 / 978-1-56145-509-6
Hoping to be more than a benchwarmer, Chris learns that defense is just as important as offense.

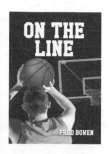

On the Line
PB: $6.95 / 978-1-56145-511-9
Marcus is the highest scorer and the best rebounder, but he's not so great at free throws—until the school custodian helps him overcome his fear of failure.

Outside Shot
PB: $6.95 / 978-1-56145-956-8
HC: $14.95 / 978-1-56145-955-1
Richie Mallon has always known he was a shooter. He practices every day at his driveway hoop, perfecting his technique. Now that he is facing basketball tryouts under a tough new coach, will his amazing shooting talent be enough to keep him on the team?

Real Hoops
PB: $6.95 / 978-1-56145-566-9
Hud can run, pass, and shoot at top speed. But he's not much of a team player. Can Ben convince Hud to leave his dazzling—but one-man—style back on the asphalt?

Double Reverse
PB: $6.95 / 978-1-56145-807-3
HC: $14.95 / 978-1-56145-814-1
The season starts off badly, and things get even worse when the Panthers quarterback is injured. Jesse knows the playbook by heart, but he feels that he's too small for the role. Can he play against type and help the Panthers become a winning team?

Quarterback Season
PB: $6.95 / 978-1-56145-594-2
Matt expects to be the starting quarterback. But after a few practices watching Devro, a talented seventh grader, he's starting to get nervous. To make matters worse, his English teacher is on his case about a new class assignment: a journal.

Touchdown Trouble
PB: $6.95 / 978-1-56145-497-6
Thanks to a major play by Sam, the Cowboys beat their archrivals to remain undefeated. But the celebration ends when Sam and his teammates make an unexpected discovery. Is their perfect season in jeopardy?

Go for the Goal!
PB: $6.95 / 978-1-56145-632-1
Josh and his talented travel league soccer teammates are having trouble coming together as a successful team—until he convinces them to try team-building exercises.

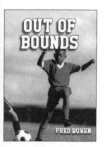

Out of Bounds
PB: $6.95 / 978-1-56145-894-3
HC: $14.95 / 978-1-56145-845-5
During a game against the Monarchs, Nate has to decide between going for a goal after a player on the rival team gets injured, or kicking the ball out of bounds as an act of good sportsmanship. What is the balance between playing fair and playing your best?

Soccer Team Upset
PB: $6.95 / 978-1-56145-495-2
Tyler is angry when his team's star player leaves to join an elite travel team. Just as Tyler expected, the Cougars' season goes straight downhill. Can he make a difference before it's too late?